Arthur and the Perfect Brother

A Marc Brown ARTHUR Chapter Book

Arthur and the Perfect Brother

Text by Stephen Krensky
Based on a teleplay by Joe Fallon

Little, Brown and Company

Boston   New York   London

First Edition

The characters and events portrayed in this book are fictitious. Any similarity to real persons, living or dead, is coincidental and not intended by the author.

Arthur® is a registered trademark of Marc Brown.

Text has been reviewed and assigned a reading level by Laurel S. Ernst, M.A., Teachers College, Columbia University, New York, New York; reading specialist, Chappaqua, New York

ISBN 0-316-12163-0 (hc)
ISBN 0-316-12226-2 (pb)
Library of Congress Catalog Card Number 00-131247

10 9 8 7 6 5 4 3 2 1

WOR (hc)
COM-MO (pb)

Printed in the United States of America

For Fred Rogers

Chapter 1

• • • • • • • • • • •

Arthur was painting a picture at the kitchen table, when his sister D.W. sneaked up behind him.

"I know you're there, D.W.," he said.

"I know I'm here, too," she answered.

Rrriinnng!

"Will you get the phone, D.W.?" asked Arthur.

"I can't." D.W. was frowning. "I'm too busy trying to figure out what you're painting."

"Will you just ANSWER THE PHONE!?"

D.W. squinted at the paper. "Is that a horse or a pig?"

"This isn't twenty questions, D.W. Go away."

"You shouldn't talk to me like that," said D.W. "I'm your sister."

"Don't remind me."

Mrs. Read entered from the living room. "Arthur, that was Alan's mother on the phone. She was just confirming his plans to stay with us this weekend."

Arthur brightened. The Brain was coming over because his parents were going on some kind of business trip. But Arthur didn't care about their trip. What he cared about was having a friend over for two whole days.

"This is going to be great!" said Arthur. "For once there'll be somebody who'll do all the things I like. It'll be like having a brother for the weekend."

Arthur imagined all the fun stuff they could do. . . .

"Are you sure this will work?" asked

Arthur, hammering the last nail into a wooden box with a glass bubble on top.

The Brain approached him wearing protective goggles and big rubber gloves. He was carrying a large glowing ball.

"Just wait until I insert the nuclear core. Will you open the door?"

Arthur swung open a small door in the side of the box and the Brain tossed the core inside it. Immediately the glass bubble began to glow.

"Okay," said the Brain, "we have ignition. Let's go."

He and Arthur stepped inside. The Brain pulled a lever and the box began to shake. Outside the bubble, houses and streets disappeared and the neighborhood became a forest.

Arthur looked at his watch. Its hands were turning backward.

"What time do you want to go home?" he asked.

"Home?" said the Brain. "That could be a

problem. I don't know how to go forward in time. Just back."

"You mean we're stuck here!?"

Outside, a crater closed up and a comet returned to space. A tyrannosaurus appeared beside them and was opening its mouth to take a big bite.

"Whoa!" said Arthur, looking around the kitchen. *Maybe it would be better to do something else,* he thought.

Inside his room, Arthur and the Brain put on suction boots. Then they walked up the walls and onto the ceiling.

D.W. entered the room. "Arthur?"

Suddenly a hairy spider dropped down in front of her face. She screamed and ran out.

Up on the ceiling, Arthur and the Brain reeled in the spider, laughing hysterically.

"Yes," said Arthur, smiling sweetly at his sister, "this will definitely be one weekend I'll never forget."

Chapter 2

• • • • • • • • • • • •

"T-minus two hours, twenty-three minutes and counting," Arthur said.

He and D.W. were getting ready for lunch in the kitchen. At the stove, their father was seasoning his Bubble Trouble Stew. He called it that in honor of the mess it always made on the stove.

"I wasn't aware of any countdowns in progress," said Mr. Read. "What's the mission?"

"It's the Brain," said Arthur. "He'll be arriving for the weekend in two hours, twenty-three, no, twenty-two minutes."

"I see. Do I still have time to change into

my tuxedo? Will I be expected to make a speech?"

"No, no," said Arthur, "nothing like that."

"Who can I have stay over for the weekend?" asked D.W.

"It's not a competition, D.W.," said her father. "Another time it will be your turn. But this weekend is Arthur's."

Arthur nodded. "And I want it to go *really* well. So you all have to be especially nice to the Brain. Make him feel at home."

His father frowned. "Arthur, isn't this the same Brain we've known for years? The one who's been here hundreds of times before?"

"Yes, but this is different," said Arthur. "It will be more like he's part of the family. And we'll be hanging around together the whole time."

"Oh, brother," said D.W.

In the den, Mrs. Read was lying on the

floor playing with Baby Kate. D.W. stomped in and plopped down in a chair. She did not look happy.

"Is something wrong, D.W.?" her mother asked.

"I'll say. It's hard enough dealing with Arthur. Once the Brain is here it'll be like having two Arthurs around."

She shuddered at the thought.

"I'm sure you'll survive," said her mother, shaking a rattle at Kate.

"Maybe."

D.W. huffed and puffed as she ran all around the living room.

"You'll never take me alive!" she cried.

There were two identical Arthurs, one on each end of the room. Each was holding strips of cloth bandages.

"Don't be silly," said Arthur #1. "We just want to play."

"You do like to play, don't you?" said

Arthur #2. "Don't you want to play Egyptian princess?"

"First, you're an Egyptian princess," said Arthur #1, "then you're a mummy."

The two Arthurs started to walk toward D.W., their arms outstretched.

"No!" cried D.W. "Go away. Mommmmm!"

D.W. stood up and rushed out of the room.

"Maybe I should spend the weekend at Grandma Thora's," she muttered. "I'm sure it would be much safer."

Chapter 3

• • • • • • • • • • • •

When the Brain got out of his family's car, Arthur and his parents were waiting in the driveway.

"You're late," said Arthur.

The Brain looked at his watch. "Only by thirty-four seconds."

"Oh, well, it seemed longer."

"Good-bye, Alan," said his mother. "Be good."

The Brain nodded.

"Thanks again for having him," she said to Mrs. Read. "Well, we're off to the Ice Creamers' convention. We'll be back late tomorrow afternoon."

"She's nominated for best new flavor," said the Brain's father. "Cucumber Crunch."

"It sounds very healthy," said Mr. Read.

As the Brain's parents drove off, Arthur turned to him. "Come on! Let's put your stuff in my room."

The Brain nodded. "If you'll excuse us," he said to Arthur's parents.

"Um, yes, of course," said Mr. Read.

"Thank you," said the Brain. He followed Arthur into the house.

"I've set up all my action figures," said Arthur as soon as they reached his room. "Take your pick."

"In a minute, Arthur." The Brain carefully unfolded his clothes from his bag.

"What are you doing?"

"Just being careful. I don't want anything to get wrinkled. There. That's better."

The Brain picked up Rat Villain as Pal poked his head in the doorway.

"Look out!" cried Rat Villain. "Beware the giant mad dog!"

Pal barked. Then he jumped on them.

"Down, Pal," said Arthur.

"How's everything going?" said Mrs. Read. She looked into the room. "We'll be eating in a few minutes. My, my, Alan, don't your clothes look neat?"

Arthur frowned, looking at his dirty laundry that was thrown here and there. "He's just trying to make a good impression."

The Brain smiled. Mrs. Read smiled back. "It's working," she said.

At dinner, Arthur couldn't eat fast enough. He shoved a forkful of food into his mouth with one hand and kept a grip on his glass with the other. The Brain, however, cut

everything up with his knife and chewed each bite carefully.

"Careful chewing leads to better digestion," he explained.

"I'm done!" Arthur shouted. "Let's go play." He pushed his chair back and jumped up.

But the Brain wasn't finished yet. Several minutes passed before he wiped his mouth with his napkin and turned to Arthur's father. "Dinner was delicious, Mr. Read. May I leave the table?"

Mr. Read shared a glance with Mrs. Read. "Of course, Alan," he said.

The Brain rose slowly and pushed his chair back. Once he was out, though, he tucked the chair back in. Then he cleared his plate and loaded it in the dishwasher.

"So what do you want to play now?" asked Arthur in the living room.

"Actually," said the Brain, "I was thinking we should do our homework first."

"Why? This is still Saturday. It's not due till Monday."

"But if we do it now," the Brain went on, "we can read ahead to next week's lessons tomorrow."

Arthur nearly fell over in shock. "Next week's lessons?"

"That sounds very sensible, Alan," said Mrs. Read from the kitchen.

"Oh, all right," said Arthur. Doing homework didn't sound like much fun, but Arthur wanted to be a good host.

So he followed the Brain upstairs in silence.

Chapter 4

• • • • • • • • • • •

Arthur was lying on the floor of his room writing in his notebook. The Brain was sitting at his desk nearby.

"Is it time yet?" asked Arthur.

The Brain shook his head. "It's only two minutes later than the last time you asked, which was three minutes later than the time before that."

"Okay, okay. I was just hoping for a break." Arthur looked down at his paper and then erased what he'd written. Why was it that something could make perfect sense in his head and then look so bad when it was put down on paper?

Abruptly, the Brain closed his book and put his papers away.

"Are you giving up?" Arthur asked.

"No, no," said the Brain. "I'm done."

"Done?" Arthur looked at his homework. "How can you be done?" He had only finished two out of the ten questions. "Can I look at your answers?"

"Do you *really* want to do that?" the Brain asked. "I mean, that won't help you learn how to do the problems yourself."

"All right, then. What if I just finish later?"

The Brain shrugged. "If you can live with the pressure of having unfinished homework hanging over your head, then it's okay with me."

They went outside to play basketball in the driveway. Arthur took a shot, and it bounced off the rim. The Brain got the rebound. He took a step out and then spun around for the fallaway jumper.

Swish!

The Brain took the ball out. As Arthur lunged for him, he dribbled through Arthur's legs and went in for the easy layup.

Swish!

That was followed by two hook shots and a backward toss over his head.

Swish! Swish! Swish!

"My game," said the Brain. "Want to play again?"

Arthur was bent over, panting. "You haven't missed yet. Maybe I'll go do my homework."

"Is it okay if I keep shooting?" the Brain asked. He sank a free throw. "I like to shoot a hundred free throws every day for practice."

"You mean you weren't just born this good?"

"No, of course not," said the Brain, sinking another shot.

By the time the Brain came back up-stairs, Arthur had done three more math problems. He was sitting on the bed with Pal.

The Brain started to get ready for bed. He changed into his pajamas and went into the bathroom to brush his teeth.

"You were gone a long time," Arthur said when he returned.

"Brushing and flossing can't be rushed," the Brain explained. He lay down on the cot and pulled the blanket up to his chin.

"I guess not," Arthur admitted. "Hey, while you were gone, I had an idea. After everyone else is asleep, do you want to sneak downstairs and watch *Curse of the Puppet Sister* on TV?"

The Brain yawned. "Wouldn't your parents get mad? Besides, it's important that we get our rest. It's while you sleep that you grow."

Arthur flopped back down on his pillow. "I'd rather be short and watch scary movies," he muttered.

But the Brain didn't hear him. He was already fast asleep.

Chapter 5

•••••••••••

When Arthur awoke the next morning, he rolled over onto his side. "Good morning, Brain," he said.

But the Brain didn't answer. He was gone.

Arthur quickly got dressed. *It isn't like the Brain to get up early,* he thought. *Where could he be?*

Arthur was just putting on his sneakers when D.W. ran in.

"Look out the window, Arthur!" she said. "While you were asleep, the Brain taught Pal a whole bunch of new tricks."

"Yeah, right, D.W.," said Arthur. "Even I have trouble getting Pal to learn tricks."

D.W. folded her arms. "See for yourself," she said.

Arthur looked out.

Down in the backyard, the Brain was giving Pal a hand signal. Pal was walking on his hind legs. At another signal, he balanced a doggy treat on his nose. After the third, Pal picked up a piece of paper and put it in the garbage can.

D.W. applauded. "I always thought that dog was dumb. But now I know better. The problem was you, Arthur."

But Arthur wasn't there. He had already turned and bolted down the stairs.

"Brain!" cried Arthur, dashing into the backyard. "How did you ever get Pal to pay attention to you?"

"It wasn't hard. The whole thing started while I was still in bed. I was having this dream where I was caught in a giant cement mixer. It was going round and round. The cement was rubbing against my face. It felt rough and wet. Then I woke up and found Pal licking my face. He seemed to want to play, and you were snoring, so—"

"I don't snore," said Arthur.

"Very well," said the Brain, "you were making heavy breathing sounds. Either way, I came outside with Pal and we started practicing. He's a very smart dog."

"I guess," said Arthur, giving Pal a sharp look.

After breakfast, Arthur and the Brain decided to build gliders in the garage. The Brain gently sanded each wing of his plane and carefully notched the tail. Arthur just slapped his together so that at least he would finish first.

At the other end of the garage, Mr. Read

was making sandwiches for one of his catering jobs. He was spreading mustard, ketchup, and mayonnaise from three large plastic bottles.

"You know, Mr. Read," said the Brain, after watching him for a few moments, "you could accomplish that more efficiently."

"Oh?" Mr. Read smiled. "I can use all the help I can get."

The Brain took a roll of tape and taped the three bottles together. Then he picked them up and squeezed them at the same time.

"That's fantastic!" said Mr. Read. "Why didn't I think of that? Isn't that great, Arthur?"

Arthur sighed. "I guess. Are you done yet, Brain? I want to show you my favorite game. It has a map and cards and one hundred thirty-four individual pieces."

"Sounds good," said the Brain. "But first I promised to help your mom with her computer."

"All right," said Arthur, trying to hide his disappointment. "I'll be waiting when you're done."

Chapter 6

• • • • • • • • • • •

Arthur set up the board game on the picnic table in the backyard. He placed all the pieces in a row and separated the cards into two piles.

"Whenever the Brain is ready, I'll be ready," he said.

But the Brain wasn't ready anytime soon.

Finally, Arthur's mother came out to do some gardening. "Arthur, I have to tell you, Alan is truly amazing. He deleted all the old files on my computer. Then he added a few things, and now the software runs faster."

"That's good," said Arthur. "So is he done now?"

"Oh, yes. I didn't want to take all his time."

"So he's coming right out?"

"I'm sure he will be—as soon as he's finished with D.W."

"D.W.?" Arthur frowned. "What's he doing with her?"

"I'm not sure. But you should be very pleased. D.W. doesn't get along with everyone, you know. And just think, you were worried about whether Alan would fit in."

Arthur sighed. He could barely remember having such a thought. It seemed like a million years ago.

His mother looked at him. "Arthur, is anything wrong?"

"Wrong? Why would you think that?"

"You have this worried look on your face."

"No, no, I'm fine. Just looking forward to playing with *my friend*, the Brain. That's not a lot to ask, is it? I mean, he did come over to spend the weekend with *me*, didn't he?"

"Of course," said Mrs. Read, "and we certainly appreciate that you're sharing him with the rest of us."

Arthur sighed. "I think I'll go see how they're doing."

He walked up to the window and listened.

"'Rapunzel, Rapunzel, let down your hair.'"

The Brain was sitting on the couch reading a story to D.W.

"She's putting all her hair out the window of the tower," the Brain explained. "It's supposed to reach down to the ground. Of course, the longest hair ever recorded only grew two hundred and six inches. Hers is at least three times that length."

"She must use truckloads of shampoo to wash it," said D.W. "But why does she do it? Drop her hair out the window, I mean."

"So that her visitor can climb up and see her." The Brain considered his statement. "However, in real life the structural integrity of hair would probably not withstand the strain. That's why this is a fairy tale."

D.W. nodded.

"Hey, Brain," Arthur called out. "The game is all set up. Are you ready?"

D.W. stood up and walked over to the window. "He can't play now. He's reading."

"Well, tell him to hurry up. Anyway, how come you never want me to read to you?" Arthur asked.

"The Brain reads faster, he does all the voices, and he's very good at explaining things."

D.W. got up and closed the curtains—right in front of Arthur's face.

"I'll be there in a minute," the Brain shouted.

Arthur wanted to believe him, he really did. But somehow he just couldn't.

Chapter 7

Buster was sitting on the balcony outside his apartment. He was practicing his detective skills, especially his powers of observation. The sky, he noticed, was blue.

"So it's not raining," he said to himself, writing in his journal.

He looked around. The tree branches were covered with green leaves.

"NOT WINTER," he wrote in big letters.

He looked around again. Someone was bicycling toward his apartment building. From a distance, it looked like Arthur. As the rider got even closer, he looked even more like Arthur.

"Hi, Buster!"

He even sounds like Arthur, thought Buster. "Arthur, is that you?"

"Yes. Who else would I be?"

Buster looked confused. "I don't know. But what are you doing here? I thought the Brain was coming over to stay at your house."

"He did."

"How come he left so early?"

Arthur took a deep breath. "He didn't leave. He's still there."

Buster gasped. "You left him *alone* with your family? What kind of friend are you?"

"Don't worry," said Arthur. "The Brain and my family are getting along fine. A little too fine, really. I think they might even be starting to like him more than they like me. He's smarter. He's neater. He even eats better."

"Eats better?" Buster looked puzzled. "How does he do that?"

"Well, last night we had stew and french fries for dinner. I'm eating the fries the usual way—"

"With your fingers?"

"Of course. But the Brain actually cuts his up with a knife and fork."

"Whoa! I don't even do that at my grandparents' house."

Arthur nodded. "I told you it was serious."

"Well, maybe," said Buster. "But Arthur, you know the Brain wouldn't try to make you look bad on purpose. He's your friend."

"I suppose. I guess it's not his fault he's so perfect."

"I'll bet he's standing in the driveway waiting for you to come back."

"Really?"

The Brain was standing at the end of Arthur's driveway with large binoculars. Every few seconds he scanned the horizon.

"Any luck?" asked Mrs. Read, appearing behind him.

The Brain shook his head. "No sign of him. No sign at all."

"Well, I made you some cookies and lemonade to keep up your strength."

"That was very thoughtful, Mrs. Read," said the Brain. "But I just couldn't enjoy them without Arthur."

"Hey, Brain!" shouted D.W. from the window. "Come read me another book."

"Sorry, D.W.," said the Brain, "but I just can't concentrate until Arthur's back safe and sound."

"Never mind about Arthur," said D.W. "He'll be fine."

"We don't know for sure," the Brain insisted. "And one friend has to look out for another."

"Maybe I should go back," said Arthur.

"That's the spirit. Keep the ball rolling! Don't give up the ship!" Buster started humming "The Star-Spangled Banner."

Arthur wheeled his bike around. "Thanks, Buster! I'll see you later."

Then he headed for home.

Chapter 8

· · · · · · · · · · · ·

When Arthur returned to his house, he didn't see anyone right away.

"I'm back," he shouted.

"Over here, Arthur," called the Brain from the backyard. He was carefully reading Arthur's game instructions and writing in a notebook.

"I had to go to Buster's for something," Arthur explained.

The Brain looked up. "Oh, you were gone? I guess I didn't notice." He looked down again. "These instructions are much too complicated. I've been rewriting them."

Suddenly, Pal came running up. He passed right by Arthur and hopped into the Brain's arms.

"Easy, Pal," said the Brain. "Could you take him, Arthur? I don't want these pages to get messed up."

"Come on, Pal," said Arthur. But Pal didn't want to move.

"Oh, there you are, Arthur," said his father, emerging from the garage. "Did you ever finish your homework?"

"Sort of. . . . Well, no. I'll go do it now."

"Good idea," said his father.

Arthur sat at his desk doing his math. *How can five problems take so long to finish?* he wondered. Of course, it *was* hard to concentrate when he could hear the rest of his family laughing outside with the Brain.

"This game was so hard to understand before," said his mother.

"But now it all makes sense," said his father.

"It's a great game," said D.W. "No wonder you recommend it. When I played with Arthur, it was boring. He didn't explain all the rules like you, Brain."

Arthur tried to return to problem #7, but he didn't get very far.

"What's going on?" asked Arthur, walking into his room.

The Brain was putting up some posters on the wall. They were part of the Famous Scientist series. Arthur recognized them as the ones the Brain had at home.

His mother was standing in front of an open suitcase on the bed. "Hello, Arthur," she said. "We were just getting ready to call you."

"Why is the Brain putting up his posters on my wall?"

Mrs. Read shrugged. "Well, Arthur, as you know, we've enjoyed having Alan stay here this weekend."

"I noticed," Arthur admitted.

"But, of course, the house really isn't big enough for another person to live here. So since

we all like Alan so much, we took a family vote and decided that he should stay and you should leave."

"WHAT!?"

"But don't worry," his mother went on, "we've already spoken to Alan's parents and they've agreed to the swap."

"But, but . . . ," Arthur sputtered.

"Did you tell him?" asked D.W., prancing in behind Arthur.

"Of course she told him," said his father, climbing the stairs. He was holding Baby Kate in his arms. "I have to tell you, Arthur, I'm really looking forward to Alan refining some of my new recipes."

"But this is all so sudden," said Arthur. "Can't we talk this over?"

"Sometimes, things just feel right," said his mother. "You'll get used to it in time."

Arthur didn't know what to say.

Chapter 9

• • • • • • • • • • • •

"Arthur, wake up."

"Huh?" Arthur raised his head from his desk.

His mother was standing over him. "You fell asleep doing your math homework."

"I did?" Arthur looked around his room. It looked the way it always did. Most important, his suitcase was still in the closet and there were no Famous Scientist posters in sight.

"We didn't want to wake you, but Alan's mother called to say they were back. It's time for him to go. Will you walk him home?"

Arthur brightened. "The Brain's leaving? Not me?"

His mother frowned. "Why would you be leaving, Arthur?"

"Well, I wouldn't. Unless I had to because you made me. But you wouldn't do that. No, of course you wouldn't. Never mind."

Mrs. Read scratched her head. "Arthur, you're not making a lot of sense."

"Um, that's okay." He stood up. "It was just a bad dream. So, where's the Brain now?"

"Downstairs. The last time I checked, he was teaching Kate the alphabet."

Arthur went down to find him. The Brain was sitting with Kate on the floor in the den.

"That's right, Kate. A . . . B . . . C . . ."

"Time to go!" said Arthur.

"All right," said the Brain, putting the blocks away. "We'll continue this another time," he added to Kate.

The rest of the family was waiting by the door.

"Alan, it's been a pleasure," said Mrs. Read.

"Your visit just flew by," said Mr. Read. "Your parents are very lucky to have a son like you."

"Yeah," said D.W. "Maybe we could work out a trade."

Arthur stepped forward. "Kids say the craziest things, don't they?" he said quickly, ushering the Brain out the door.

"I guess so. Bye, everyone. Thank you very much, Mr. and Mrs. Read, for your wonderful hospitality."

He and Arthur walked together down to the corner.

"You know, Arthur," said the Brain, "it's

still early. Want to come over to my house? We could make popcorn."

"No, I don't think so." Arthur looked at the ground. "I still have a couple of those math problems to do."

"Couldn't you do them later?"

Arthur pretended to look shocked. "Put off doing homework? What kind of student do you think I am?"

"Okay, okay, I get it. But, um, you're not mad at me, are you, Arthur?"

"Who could be mad at you? You're the perfect son, the perfect brother, the perfect everything!"

"I am?"

Arthur folded his arms. "I'm sure you wish you could have stayed longer."

The Brain blushed.

"Aha!" said Arthur. "I thought so."

"It's not that," said the Brain.

"Well, then, what is it?"

"Promise you won't laugh?"

Arthur nodded.

"I'm a little homesick."

"Homesick? How can you be homesick? You had a great time from the first moment you got to my house."

"I know, Arthur. But it's still your house and your family. I miss mine."

"You do?"

The Brain nodded.

Suddenly, Arthur felt much better. "Hmmmm . . . popcorn, you said?"

"With butter, if you want it."

"All right," said Arthur. "What are we waiting for?"

Chapter 10

· · · · · · · · · · · ·

The Brain's mother was waiting at the front door when the boys arrived.

"Welcome home, Alan," she said, giving him a big kiss. "Did you have fun? I hope you weren't any trouble to the Reads."

"I don't think so."

"He was the perfect guest," said Arthur.

"Well, that's nice to hear," said the Brain's mother.

"And when I say perfect," Arthur added, "I mean *perfect*."

"Don't listen to him," said the Brain. "You know how Arthur likes to exaggerate." He dropped his bag on the hall floor and started to walk away.

"Alan?"

The Brain turned. "Okay, okay." He picked up the bag. "Um, we're going to my room to put this stuff away."

The Brain led the way up the stairs. When he got to his room, he walked right in. But Arthur paused in the doorway.

"I don't believe this!" Arthur said.

Clothes, books, and toys were spread around like confetti after a big parade.

"You don't believe what?"

Arthur waved his arm at the mess in front of him. "How can your room look like it exploded or something? You were so neat at my house."

"I know, and it almost killed me."

Arthur's jaw dropped as the Brain emptied out his clothes into a mound on the floor.

"Then that wasn't the new-and-improved you?"

"No. Just the old being-a-guest-in-somebody-else's-house me."

Arthur looked very relieved.

"Want some popcorn now?" the Brain asked.

"Okay!"

As they sat in the kitchen listening to the popcorn pop, the Brain's father arrived at the back door with some groceries.

Arthur jumped up to open the door for him. "Need any help?" he asked.

"Why, thank you, Arthur." The Brain's father gave his son a look. "I hope you're paying attention, Alan. You could learn a few things from your friend."

Arthur and the Brain just stared at each other. Then they both burst out laughing.